Dear Parents,

Welcome to the Scholastic Reader series. We [...] years of experience with teachers, parents, and children and put it into a program that is designed to match your child's interests and skills.

Level 1—Short sentences and stories made up of words kids can sound out using their phonics skills and words that are important to remember.

Level 2—Longer sentences and stories with words kids need to know and new "big" words that they will want to know.

Level 3—From sentences to paragraphs to longer stories, these books have large "chunks" of texts and are made up of a rich vocabulary.

Level 4—First chapter books with more words and fewer pictures.

It is important that children learn to read well enough to succeed in school and beyond. Here are ideas for reading this book with your child:

- Look at the book together. Encourage your child to read the title and make a prediction about the story.
- Read the book together. Encourage your child to sound out words when appropriate. When your child struggles, you can help by providing the word.
- Encourage your child to retell the story. This is a great way to check for comprehension.
- Have your child take the fluency test on the last page to check progress.

Scholastic Readers are designed to support your child's efforts to learn how to read at every age and every stage. Enjoy helping your child learn to read and love to read.

— **Francie Alexander**
Chief Education Officer
Scholastic Education

Dedicated to Aunt Katherine and the Red Sox.
With thanks to Paul Dengler,
president of Philipstown Little League, Inc.
and Jesse Merandy
—J.M.
To Nick and Sam Brown
—T.K.

Text copyright © 1999 by Jean Marzollo.
Illustrations copyright © 1999 by True Kelley.
Fluency activities copyright © 2003 Scholastic Inc.
All rights reserved. Published by Scholastic Inc.
SCHOLASTIC, CARTWHEEL BOOKS, and associated logos
are trademarks and/or registered trademarks of Scholastic Inc.

Library of Congress Cataloging-in-Publication Data is available.

ISBN: 0-590-38398-1

10 9 8 7 6 5 4 3   05 06 07
Printed in the U.S.A. 23 • First printing, April 1999

Baseball BROTHERS

by **Jean, Dan, and Dave Marzollo**
Illustrated by **True Kelley**

Scholastic Reader — Level 3

SCHOLASTIC INC.

Cartwheel B·O·O·K·S ®

New York Toronto London Auckland Sydney
Mexico City New Delhi Hong Kong Buenos Aires

"Nice day for a game," said Timmy's mom.

"Nice day to win," said Timmy's brother Ben.

They were riding in the car. Ben was in the front seat. He was thirteen.

"Can I have my glove?" asked Timmy.

"It's *my* glove," said Ben. He smacked his
fist into the glove. "I'm just letting you use
it."

"Ben's glove will give you good luck," said
their dad.

"He needs it," said Lizzie. She was older,
too. She was ten.

At the field, Ben gave Timmy his glove.

Timmy played for the Red Sox. Mr. Hernandez was the coach. He said, "Timmy, you're playing right field."

Timmy walked way out to right field.
Lizzie was feeding ducks nearby.

The Blue Jays were up. Daisy was at bat. In Timmy's town, there was no pitching in tee ball. But the teams had pitchers and catchers to field balls. Mr. Hernandez stood next to the pitcher to coach his team.

"Play ball!" yelled the umpire.

Daisy had to hit the ball off the tee. The ball had to go past the yellow rope to be in play.

Daisy hit the ball past the rope. She ran
to first base.

Wow, thought Timmy. Daisy was lucky.
She hit the ball right away. Timmy had
never hit the ball on the first swing.

The next batter was Bret. He hit the ball,
too. But not on the first swing. It took him
longer.

Timmy looked down. A butterfly had landed near his foot. He bent over to get a closer look. It was orange and black.

Slowly, slowly, s-l-o-w-l-y, Timmy reached out his hand. The butterfly walked onto his finger.

Timmy heard people screaming. He stood up. The butterfly flew off. Timmy started to chase it. Suddenly he heard Ben. Ben had run out to be near right field.

"Timmy, get the ball! Get the ball!"

Timmy looked around. He found the ball in the grass. He picked it up.

"Throw it! Throw it!"

Timmy threw it, but he was too late. The batter was on second base.

GET THE BALL!

"Are you going to use my glove or just wear it?" yelled Ben.

Timmy was embarrassed. He smacked his fist into Ben's glove. It was hard to play right field. Very few balls were ever hit out that far. That's why it was so hard to pay attention. But he would pay attention. He really would. He would be just like Ben.

He watched a Blue Jay try to hit the ball off the tee. It took a long time. Timmy watched every swing. He was really paying attention. The batter was finally put out. The next batter took a long time, too.

TOOT! TOOT! Train tracks ran behind the field. *TOOT! TOOT!* A train was coming. Timmy turned to count the cars. One, two, three, four, five...

"Timmy, turn around!" yelled Ben. "Watch the trains later!"

Timmy was scared. "Is the ball out here again?" he asked.

"No," said Ben. "Lucky for you. Now, come on. The inning's over. You're up first."

Timmy loved to bat. It was better than playing in the outfield. At bat you were doing something. He selected the biggest bat. Maybe he would get a hit on his first swing, just like Daisy.

"Let's go, Timmy," chanted his teammates. "Let's go, Timmy."

Timmy stepped into the batter's box. He took a swing at the ball.

WHOOSH! Timmy's bat swung through the air. It didn't hit anything.

"Keep your eye on the ball," said Mr. Hernandez.

Timmy looked at the little white ball sitting on the black tee. He swung again.

BONG! Timmy hit the tee. It fell over.

"You can do it. I know you can,"
yelled Ben.

The umpire put the ball back on the tee.

Everyone was quiet now. Timmy wanted
to hit the ball more than anything in the
world.

He swung. *Bam!* He hit it! The ball started
rolling toward the yellow rope.

"Run, Timmy, run!" shouted his teammates.

Timmy started running to first base. He had gotten a hit. But what if it wasn't a hit? What if the ball didn't reach the rope?

Timmy turned to look.

"Run, Timmy!" everyone shouted.

Timmy saw Blue Jays running to get the ball. The ball was past the rope!

Timmy was almost to first base. "Please don't throw me out," he wished.

The first baseman jumped to catch the ball.

Timmy reached the base. The first baseman landed. He looked into his glove. There was no ball.

Timmy was safe!

The first baseman took off after the ball. Timmy smiled. It was fun to watch someone else run after a ball.

"Timmy, keep going! Run to second base!" Ben shouted.

Timmy started to run. He could get a double! Timmy had never hit a double.

Bret was the second baseman on the Blue Jays. He was big and strong. He had one foot on the bag. His arm was stretched out to catch the ball.

Timmy ran as fast as he could. The ball fell to the ground in front of Bret. Bret tried to scoop it up. But it went between his legs!

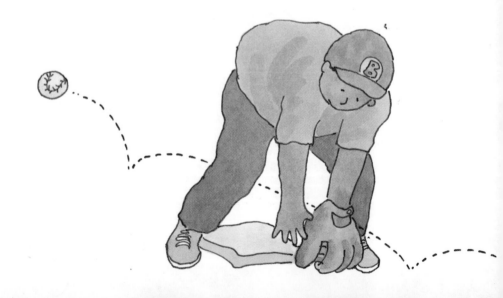

The ball bounced into the outfield. Bret chased after it.

Timmy stood on second base. He folded his arms across his chest. He had never felt so proud.

"Don't stop, Timmy. Keep running! Go to third!" everyone yelled.

Timmy started running. A triple? Was it possible?

"Go, Timmy, go!" shouted his teammates.

"Hurry, Timmy, hurry!" cheered his mom.

GO!

Timmy looked for Steve. Steve was the third baseman for the Blue Jays. Where was he? He wasn't there. He was chasing the ball, too!

The Blue Jays coach was yelling, "Steve, Steve, get back on base!"

Steve ran back to third. But Timmy got there before him.

"Keep going!" yelled Ben. "They don't have the ball yet. You can make it home!"

Timmy kept going. He ran as fast as he could. The catcher for the Blue Jays was holding up his mitt.

Timmy wanted to know where the ball was. But he was afraid to turn around. He was running so fast! He had to keep going!

"Please, please, please don't throw me out!" he said. He was so close to home.

Everyone was screaming. The Red Sox, the Blue Jays, his mother, his father, his brother, his sister.

Should he slide? Timmy had never slid into home base. He had never slid into *any* base.

But now Timmy had to slide. He jumped up. He kicked his right foot under his bottom. He stuck his left foot out as far as it would go.

OOF! He landed on his hip. Dust flew. He
got dirt in his mouth. His elbow hurt, but it
didn't matter. He was on home plate!

"Safe!" said the umpire.

Timmy stood up. He had gotten an
inside-the-park home run! His teammates
hugged him. Mr. Hernandez shook his hand.

"That was some great base-running," said
his dad.

Timmy's mom took his picture.

"You know," said Lizzie, "you really didn't
need to slide. The ball was still in the
outfield."

"But it was a great slide," said Ben. "Now
your uniform is dirty. That's cool."

The Red Sox scored three more runs before the inning was over. The score was 4–2. The Blue Jays came up to bat. The Red Sox took the field.

Timmy grabbed his brother's glove. He ran out to right field. This time he was really going to pay attention. He was going to be a great baseball player.

The first Blue Jay batter was Sarah. She took a long time at bat. Finally, she got on base.

The next batter was Gary. He couldn't hit the ball off the tee. Timmy counted the swings he took.

One, two, three, four, five, six, seven, eight...

Timmy looked down. Another butterfly had landed near his foot. It was orange and black, too. Timmy bent down to get a closer look. Was it the same one?

"Timmy! Get the ball!" yelled Ben. Timmy looked up. The ball was coming. He ran for it. Thanks to his brother, he was back in the game.